In memory of Adam and for Richard, with love   L.E.
For Teresa Cole   P.D.

Library of Congress Cataloging-in-Publication Data

Ely, Lesley
Looking after Louis / written by Lesley Ely ; illustrated by Polly Dunbar.
p. cm.
Summary: When a new boy with autism joins their classroom,
the children try to understand his world and to include him in theirs.
ISBN 0-8075-4746-8
[1. Autism—Fiction. 2. Schools—Fiction.] I. Dunbar, Polly, ill. II. Title.
P7.E556Lo2004   [E]—dc21 2003050195

Originally published in the United Kingdom in 2004 by Frances Lincoln Ltd

For more information about Albert Whitman & Company,
please visit our web site at www.albertwhitman.com.

Looking after Louis

Written by Lesley Ely
Illustrated by Polly Dunbar

ALBERT WHITMAN & COMPANY
Morton Grove, Illinois

Looking

at —

There's a new boy at school called Louis. Louis sits next to me and I look after him. He's not quite like the rest of us. Sometimes I wonder what he's thinking about. He often just sits and stares at the wall. If I ask him what he's looking at, he says, "Looking at," and keeps on looking.

I show him my pictures and I say, "Try these crayons, Louis."

He says, "Try these crayons, Louis."

Then he draws very carefully so I say, "That's good."

But I don't know what his pictures are about.

Em and I look after Louis at recess. He runs in and out of the boys' soccer game with his arms out like a ballet dancer.

Em and I thought he was playing soccer at first, but he wasn't. He just likes running inside the game. The boys get mad, but Louis doesn't notice.

Sometimes Miss Owlie says, "No soccer allowed today,"
and the soccer players stand around and don't know what to do.
Then boys and girls play together for a change.

Last no-soccer day, we let our friend Sam get on the big tire
with us. He wobbled, but we didn't laugh.

Louis was standing really still, just watching, so I called out,
"Do you want to come on the tire, Louis?"
Louis said, "Come on the tire, Louis."
But he didn't move.

Come
on the
tire,
Louis

Louis sometimes talks in the wrong place.

Yesterday Miss Owlie said, "Sit up straight, everybody."

Louis said, "Sit up straight, everybody."

We all laughed because he sounded just like Miss Owlie. She wasn't angry, though. Neither was Mrs. Kumar, who sits by Louis and helps him. They would have been angry if Em or Sam or I had done that.

At recess this morning, Sam was showing off with his new soccer ball.

Mrs. Kumar said, "Sam has magic feet!"

Louis watched Sam's feet closely. Sam said, "Do you want to play a game, Louis?"

Louis said, "Game, Louis."

Sam dribbled the ball all around the playground and Louis ran after him. Sam passed the ball to Louis. Louis didn't get it, but Sam kept it going and Louis chased it with his arms out.

Other boys joined in. If Louis's foot even touched the ball, Sam shouted, "Great game, Louis!"

Louis almost smiled.

Louis drew a picture all afternoon. Every time he used
a different color, he said, "Great game."

When he'd used every color, he stopped.

I said, "Show it to Miss Owlie," and I took him to her desk.

I said, "I think Louis's picture is about soccer."

Miss Owlie looked carefully. "Let's ask the expert!" she said.

So I got Sam.

Great
game

Sam looked at Louis's picture.
Then he said, "That's the game!
That's you! That's me! That's the ball!"
"That's the ball," Louis said.

That's
the
ba

Just then the sun shone in.
It shone through the classroom
window.

Sam said, "Can Louis and I go outside and practice soccer again, Miss Owlie?"

Miss Owlie's eyes crinkled up. She said, "Would you like to play soccer, Louis?"

Play soccer,
Louis
(

Mrs. Kumar started to take off her apron and put on her coat.

I think she knew what Louis would say.

"Play soccer, Louis," said Louis.

Miss Owlie smiled at Mrs. Kumar. "How did we guess?" she said.

Sam and Louis WHOOSHED out of our
classroom like water down a drain!

Mrs. Kumar followed them. She had a ball
in her pocket already.

"You NEVER let US play outside when it's not recess," I said.

Miss Owlie was smiling, but I wasn't. Not even a little bit.

I put my hands on my hips.

"Sam and Louis are lucky ducks today, Miss Owlie," I said.

Miss Owlie's eyes twinkled, and she got dimples in both cheeks.

"So they are," she whispered. "What do you think about it?"

She looked at me as if she expected my answer
to be very wise. So I thought extra-hard before
I whispered back, "I think we're allowed to break
rules for special people."

Miss Owlie put her finger to her lips and nodded
a tiny little nod that nobody saw but me.

We peeped through the classroom window at
Sam and Louis's Great Game . . .

and I felt special, too.

LOUIS, the main character in this story, has a developmental disorder known as autism. Autism is characterized by severe impairment in communication and social interaction and a markedly restricted range of interests and activities. Diagnosis has been on the rise, probably because the symptoms are now better understood.

Many autistic children do best in special classrooms tailored to their needs. However, high-functioning children can be taught in a regular classroom. Education of children with disabilities in regular classrooms is often called "inclusion" or "mainstreaming."

In this story, Louis is being taught in a regular class. A sympathetic, flexible teacher sets a mood of tolerance and encourages him to connect with his classmates. Some children with autism, like Louis, also have individual aides who give the extra attention that helps the children be part of the classroom world.

This story highlights the advantages of inclusion for both disabled children and their regular education classmates. Louis is able to watch and learn from his peers and to practice social skills, while his classmates learn empathy and respect for individual differences. In the end, all come to enjoy each other's unique strengths.

Kori Levos Skidmore, Ph.D.
Child Clinical Psychologist

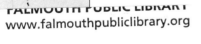